Stella Batts

Something Blue

Stella Batts

Something Blue

Book

Courtney Sheinmel

Illustrated by Jennifer A. Bell

For Mr. & Mrs. Philip M. Getter

—Courtney

To V and S

—Jennifer

Sleeping Bear Press™

315 East Eisenhower Parkway, Suite 200 • Ann Arbor, MI 48108 • www.sleepingbearpress.com
© Sleeping Bear Press

PURELL® is a registered trademark of GOJO Industries, Inc. Bubble Wrap® is a registered trademark of Sealed Air Corporation. Lucky Charms® is a registered trademark of General Mills Inc. Fruit Loops® is a trademark of Kellogg Company.

Printed and bound in the United States.
10 9 8 7 6 5 4 3 2 1

Library of Congress Cataloging-in-Publication Data • Sheinmel, Courtney. • Stella Batts: something blue • written by Courtney Sheinmel, illustrated by Jennifer A. Bell. • pages cm. — • (Stella Batts ; book 6) • Summary: "Stella and her family drive to Los Angeles to attend her aunt Laura's wedding. Stella is excited to be a flower girl but things don't go as planned. She accidently sprays paint on her aunt's wedding dress and the daughter of the man marrying Aunt Laura wants to run away"— • Provided by publisher. • ISBN 978-1-58536-851-8 (hard cover) — ISBN 978-1-58536-852-5 (paperback) • [1. Weddings—Fiction. 2. Flower girls—Fiction. 3. Family life—California—Fiction.] • I. Bell, Jennifer (Jennifer A.), 1977-illustrator. • II. Title. III. Title: Something blue. • PZ7.S54124Su 2014 • [Fic]—dc23 • 2013024898

Table of Contents

Knock, Knock

"Hey, Stella," my friend Talisa called. It was Friday at noon. School was out early for the weekend because of teacher conferences, and I was walking to Mr. King's car. He's my friend Evie's dad, and he was driving carpool that day.

I turned back toward Talisa. "What?" I asked.

"Will you remember me in a second?"

"Yup," I said.

"What about in a minute?"

"I'll remember you in a minute, too," I told her.

"Will you remember me when you go away this weekend, to your aunt's wedding?"

"Sure," I said.

"And when you're back home?" she asked.

"Of course I will," I told her.

"Knock, knock," she said.

"Who's there?" I asked.

"Oh no, you forgot me already!"

CHAPTER 1

Presents

Mr. King drove my sister, Penny, and me to Batts Confections after school instead of home, because that's where Mom was waiting for us. Batts Confections is our family store, in case you forgot or you haven't read my other books. And it's not just any kind of store—it's the *best* kind of store. A *candy* store.

Mom was waiting on the sidewalk for us. My baby brother, Marco, was in her arms. Penny and I said good-bye to everyone in the car and climbed out.

It was good to spend a little time with Marco, because he wouldn't be coming to Los Angeles with us. That's where we were going, because Aunt Laura was getting married there—she's Mom's younger sister. We were staying at a hotel, and Mom said it would be too many people with too many germs for such a little baby.

Mom gave me Purell to squirt on my hands and clean off all the germs from school, and then she let me hold Marco so I could show him some of my favorite Batts Confections things. "This is the candy circus that I helped set up," I said.

"I helped too!" Penny added.

"And those are the candy lions and zebras, and the cotton-candy machine," I told him. I know he's just a baby, but he smiled

and made his happy baby sounds, so maybe he understood a little bit.

"Now let's go upstairs and show him the party room!" Penny said.

"There's a leak upstairs," Mom said. "I don't want you girls up there. Besides, Dad has a surprise for you."

"Ooh, goody! I love surprises!" Penny said. "Is it that we never have to clean our rooms again?"

Mom laughed. "Nope, not even close," she said.

"Is it about us being in the wedding?" I asked.

Mom shook her head.

"We already knew about that anyway," Penny told me. "Is it about our cousin?" she asked Mom.

Penny and I were getting a cousin at the wedding. That's because Aunt Laura's soon-to-be husband, our soon-to-be Uncle Rob, had been married before and he had a daughter named Lia. Penny and I had never had a cousin. Dad's an only child, so we don't have any uncles or aunts on his side of the family. Mom has Aunt Laura, but so far she hasn't had any kids.

"But we already know about Lia, too," I reminded Penny.

"Oh yeah," said Penny.

"So what is it?" I asked.

"We'll go downstairs so you can see," Mom said. She took Marco back from me. They went down the stairs, because Mom hates elevators. But Penny likes elevators, and so do I. I pressed the button for it to come pick the two of us up. When the doors opened, we stepped inside. My finger was on the button marked "C." C stands for cellar, which is another word for basement. Penny called out, "I claim getting to press the button for the floor!"

"Too late, I already pressed it," I told her, pressing the button right at that second.

"That's not fair!" Penny said. We rode

down and the doors opened. "I'm telling!" Penny called, and she raced ahead of me.

Sometimes little sisters are SUPER annoying.

"Stella did a mean wrong thing!" Penny said, as soon as she walked through the office door. "She pressed the outside elevator button. Then she pressed the inside elevator button."

"So?" I asked. "There's no rule against that."

"There is too, because it's not fair," Penny whined. "I didn't get to press any button!"

"Are we going to keep talking about buttons, or are we going to check out the surprise?" Dad asked.

Dad always changes the subject when he wants to distract Penny, and it always works.

"Where is it?" Penny asked.

"Right here," Dad said, moving toward a

big brown box in the corner. He pulled down the front flap so we could all see. Penny and I breathed in deep at the exact same time, and let it out at the same time: "Oooooh."

This is what was inside the box: a giant candy wedding cake.

"It's for Aunt Laura," Mom explained, even though she didn't have to—I figured that out all by myself. It looked more delicious than any cake I'd ever seen, and it also looked taller than any cake I'd ever seen.

"How many floors are there?" Penny asked.

"Floors?" Dad asked.

"You know, floors of cake."

"Oh, you mean tiers," Dad said. "Count them up."

I counted quickly in my head: five. But Penny counted slowly, out loud: "One, two, three, four, five. There are five!" she said.

"That's right," Dad told her.

Each tier was covered in vanilla frosting and had a different candy theme. Here, I'll list them for you, from bottom to top.

1. The biggest tier was filled with Marco's Minis. That's a new thing Penny invented after Marco was born, so he'd have something named for him at the store. There were mini chocolate bars, itty-bitty peanut butter cups, tiny cookie dough balls, and a whole lot more.

2. The second tier was covered with dots—you know, those sugar dots that come on a big piece of paper and you eat them off. Well, these dots were stuck right onto the frosting—which I bet tastes even better.

3. The third tier was all jelly beans, in the same colors as the dots, wrapped around the middle tier like a big ribbon tying up the whole cake.

4. There were more jelly beans on the fourth tier, but these were white and looked like pearls.

5. Finally, the top tier was a cupcake,

and at the tippy-top of the cupcake there were marzipan sculptures that I think were supposed to be Aunt Laura and her fiancé, Rob, but it didn't look too much like them. The whole thing looked amazing anyhow. And I told Dad.

"It's a pretty good present for the bride and groom, huh?" Dad asked.

"Yeah," Penny said. "It looks tasty and delicious."

"It looks perfect," I said.

"How is it getting to Los Angeles?" Penny asked.

"Stuart and I are going to pack it up ourselves," Dad said. "We'll put extra bubble wrap around it. It'll go in the backseat between you two on the drive down. That way you girls can make sure nothing happens to it."

"I'll put a seat belt around the box," I said.

"And I'll make sure it doesn't get bumped at all."

"I knew I could count on you," Dad said.

"I have to tell you something," Penny told him.

"What's that?"

"I don't want to have a cake for my wedding present. Then I'd have to share it with everyone else, and then it will be all eaten up and I won't have anything left to play with."

"Are you getting married anytime soon?" Dad asked.

"Not yet," Penny said. "But one day—Maverick and I are going to get married when we're all grown up." Maverick is our neighbor. He's six and a half years old, and he gave Penny her very favorite stuffed animal ever, her duck-billed platypus, Belinda.

"So that gives us a little time to work on

your sharing skills," Mom told Penny. "But when it comes to Aunt Laura, we got her something from the registry in addition to making the wedding cake."

"What's a registry?" I asked.

"It's a list you make when you're getting married—a wish list of all the things you want for your new life together," Mom said.

"Oh, I can't wait to be a grown-up," Penny

said. "You get to use the sharp knives, and you don't have a bedtime, and you get to tell people what to buy you!"

"But that's a family present," I said. "Everyone knows that a family present means it's really from the grown-ups and not the kids. I want to get her something from me."

"You're going to be her flower girl," Mom told me.

"And me too!" Penny interjected.

"Right, both of you girls. And your presence is your present."

"What does that mean?" Penny asked.

"It means just being there is enough," Mom told her.

But that didn't seem like enough to me. "I have my allowance money at home," I said. "I can get her something with that."

"But, Stel," Mom said, "I thought you

were saving up for something for yourself."

"I was saving up to get something," I said. "I'm not sure what yet, so maybe this is it."

"Oh, darling," Dad said. "That is so generous of you. I'm really proud of you."

"I'm proud of you, too," Mom told me.

"I want to get something for Aunt Laura, too," Penny said, which was totally copying me, by the way.

"Tell you what," Mom said. "The registry is on the computer. We can pull it up right now—I'll put it on my credit card, and you'll pay me back when we get home. Okay?"

"Okay!" I said.

"Okay!" echoed Penny.

There's a computer right on the desk in Mom and Dad's office, so Mom turned it on and typed a few things to get to the registry Web site. Penny and I leaned over Mom's shoulder. I read the items out loud, because Penny couldn't read them herself: picture frames, vases, pots and pans. All kinds of boring stuff. And also, it was all pretty expensive. Like the vase cost a HUNDRED dollars. "There's nothing I can get," I told

Mom. "Except for a fork. And who wants to get one fork as a present?"

"Penny can buy the knife," Mom said. "Then it's a set."

"Actually I decided I don't need to get Aunt Laura my own present," Penny said. "Because I really don't have any of my own money, and I'm going to sing Aunt Laura a song as a present."

Dad said that was a great idea, but singing isn't a real present either, which meant Penny wasn't so good at sharing after all.

"I still want to buy something, but not on this list." No offense to Aunt Laura, but if I was making a list of presents for people to get me, I wouldn't pick any of the same things! In fact, I was surprised that Aunt Laura picked such boring stuff, because she's not boring at all.

Want to know how not boring she is? Every time I see her, her ponytail is a different color! It's one of the reasons why it's so fun to see her, because it's a surprise every time.

"Can we go to the mall and I can pick something out there?" I asked.

"I'm afraid we don't have time, sweets," Mom said. "We've got to get Marco settled with Mrs. Miller, and then get on the road."

"You can share my song with me," Penny said. She started to sing. "We're going to be flower girls, flower girls. All three of us will be wearing pearls, wearing pearls."

"We're not wearing pearls," I told her.

"I know," she said. "But it's a song so it's okay if it's not all true, right?"

"Oh, absolutely," Dad said.

"Now your turn," Penny told me.

"Okay," I said. After all, a wrong song

for a present is better than no present at all. I thought for just a second and then I sang: "Ooh, this weekend, the sun will shine. We'll walk down the aisle in a straight line!"

CHAPTER 2

Welcome to the Hotel Aoife

It takes four hours to drive from Somers, where we live, to Los Angeles. I planned to write a bit in my book during the drive, but right when I pulled out my notebook, there was a bump in the road, and I accidentally knocked into the cake box.

"Everything okay back there?" Mom asked.

"Yes," Penny and I said at the same time.

"Jinx!" I cried.

"Hey, Stella," Penny said.

"You can't talk," I reminded her. "Not until I say your name backwards."

"But I have to ask you something really, REALLY important."

"Let her talk," Dad said. "Otherwise it will be an even longer ride."

"Batts Jane Penelope," I said.

"Let's play I Spy," Penny said.

"We can't," I told her. "The cake box is too tall between us, so we can't see the same things."

"How much longer will this ride be?" Penny asked.

"A bit longer," Mom said.

"When we get to the hotel, will we get to meet Lia right away?" I asked.

"I'm not sure," Mom said. "We're running on the late side already."

It had taken awhile for Mom to give Mrs. Miller all the instructions for taking care of Marco. Then Penny and I had to give her instructions for taking care of Fudge and Penny Jr. Those are our fish, and Mrs. Miller was taking care of them, too.

"We have to check in and we'll want to drop everything in the room and do a quick washup, and then it's off to the rehearsal dinner," Mom said. "But you'll definitely see Lia there."

"We have to rehearse eating dinner?" Penny asked.

"No, that's just what it's called," Mom said. "But we're really rehearsing the wedding part of things."

"We get to practice being flower girls?" Penny cried. "That's so cool! It's like a play!"

"It *is* cool," said Dad. "Now how about a different car game? Geography?"

But Penny didn't want to play that game because she thinks it's too hard. Mom and Dad started talking about grown-up things. After awhile I closed my eyes, not because I was really tired, but because there wasn't anything else to do. I must have fallen asleep, because I didn't wake up until Dad said, "Girls, we're here."

We pulled into a circular driveway and we were met at the curb by a man in a navy suit. I knew his name right away, Lawrence, because it was stitched just above the pocket on his blazer. He said, "Welcome to the Hotel Aoife!" pronouncing it differently than I expected. Like this: A-fee. Then he took our bags and put them on a rolling cart, so we wouldn't have to carry them.

"Come," Mom said.

"What about our car?" I asked.

"They'll park it for us," she told me. "It's called valet."

That was the first amazing thing about the hotel. There were a whole lot more.

Inside the lobby, other people were

wearing the same outfit as Lawrence. I guessed it was the uniform for everyone who worked at the hotel. There were people *not* wearing the uniform, too—they had to be other guests. I didn't see Aunt Laura, or Soon-to-be Uncle Rob, or Grandpa, or Grandma, or anyone else I recognized.

But here's what I did see: a pond right INSIDE the lobby of the hotel. Actually it was so big it may have even been a lake. There were fish swimming in it—big ones, like ten times the size of Fudge and Penny Jr. In the center, there was a giant statue of a fish, with water spitting out of its mouth and back into the pond.

Mom and Dad were at the front desk, where a woman named Marcie (that's the name that was sewn into her blazer) was checking us in. She said we'd be staying in Room 2118, on

the twenty-first floor. Instead of keys, Marcie gave Dad little credit cards with the name of the hotel on them. She pointed us to the elevator, right behind the fountain. Lawrence was taking a different elevator, with our bags. I don't know why the bags couldn't go in the same elevator as the guests, but Dad said that was just the rule.

Our elevator opened up right as we walked up to it. It had windows all around. I pressed the button for floor twenty-one. "No fair!" said Penny. "I was going to claim pressing the button." She stepped forward and pressed other buttons—floor two and floor four—which weren't our floors, of course.

She would've pressed even more buttons, but Mom said, "That's enough, Pen."

"Mom, you're in an elevator!" I said.

"I don't mind this one because of all of the windows," she explained.

The door opened on the second floor. "It smells like pool!" Penny exclaimed.

"That's because there's an indoor pool," Dad said. "You can explore it later." He pressed the "door close" button. Two seconds later we stopped on floor four, and Dad did the same thing. The doors closed again and we zoomed up, up, up, all the way to the twenty-first floor.

Ding!

I'd never been so high up in my whole entire life, and we were going to be sleeping up there for the whole weekend! The hallway outside the elevator looked like it went on for a whole mile.

"This is the best hotel I've ever been to!" Penny cried.

It was the only hotel she'd ever been to, but I didn't say that because I actually agreed with her. It was my first hotel too, and I couldn't think of any hotel that could ever be better.

"Let's skip the whole way down to our room!" Penny said.

We skipped, and Mom and Dad walked behind us. Dad let us into the room with the credit card key.

Lawrence hadn't yet arrived with our bags, which meant we had time to explore before we had to get ready. Here's what we found: a bedroom area for Mom and Dad, and another bedroom area for Penny and me. Both beds had free chocolates waiting for us on the pillows!

On the table, there was a binder that had a menu of all the food you could order, and it would be delivered right there to your room. In the bathroom, hanging on the back of the door, there were the softest, thickest, coziest bathrobes I'd ever seen. On the counter there was soap in the shape of eensy weensy fish, plus loads of other stuff. "Mom, are we allowed to use all this stuff?" I called.

"Yes," she said. "It's complimentary." Complimentary means free.

"I claim the fish soap!" I said.

"I claim the toothpaste!" Penny cried.

"I claim the dental floss!" I said.

"I claim whatever is in this box," Penny said. "What is it?"

She handed it to me to read: "A shower cap," I said. "I don't even want it."

There was a phone, too—a phone in the bathroom!—and more phones in each of the bedroom areas. Each one had a list of instructions stuck to the receiver: "Press 1 to reach the front desk. Press 2 to reach the concierge."

"Hey, Dad, look at this," I said, pointing to the option for Press 9: Ask Aoife Anything. "Can I really ask *anything*?"

"What sort of question do you have in mind?"

"I haven't thought of one yet."

There was a knock on the door. Lawrence had arrived with the bags. We unpacked quickly and got ready. Then we had to go back downstairs, to Ballroom A, because that's where the rehearsal was happening.

For the wedding itself, Penny and I were going to wear fancy flower-girl dresses. They were exactly the same, light purple with darker purple sashes around the middle, except mine was a couple sizes bigger. But this rehearsal wasn't a dress rehearsal, like you have if you're in a play, so we didn't get to wear them yet. "We're saving them for the real deal," Mom told us.

We still had to look nice for the rehearsal, since it was in a ballroom. Plus, we were going to be meeting our soon-to-be cousin for the first time, and seeing lots of relatives, and posing for a whole bunch of pictures. Penny wore the pink dress from her friend Zoey's birthday, and I wore a red skirt and top, with my brown moccasin boots.

But when we got down to the ballroom, it was just . . . a room. A big room for sure, but still really plain. The carpet was plain beige, and the walls were plain white. Off to one side of the room there were a bunch of tables, and they didn't even have tablecloths on them. There was a piano against the wall—the only non-beige thing in the room. It was black.

On the other side of the room, a group of people stood in a huddle. I recognized the backs of Grandma and Grandpa's heads . . . and could that be Aunt Laura next to them? I wasn't sure. It sort of looked like her, but her hair was pulled back into a plain brown ponytail, no color. She was wearing a plain beige skirt and a cream-colored top, so she matched the room.

"Hello!" Penny called.

"Laura!" Mom said, moving forward, her arms stretched out to hug her.

But when Aunt Laura turned around, her face was blotchy red, like maybe she'd been crying. I'd never seen a grown-up cry before. "Lia's missing," she said.

CHAPTER 3

Lost and Found

"Missing?" Mom said. "What do you mean missing?"

"She came in here with Rob, not twenty minutes ago," Aunt Laura said. "We were standing right here, going over last-minute wedding details. When Rob looked up, she was gone!"

I moved closer to Mom's side and reached for her hand. She took mine and squeezed tight.

"She probably just stepped out to go to

the bathroom or to explore," Grandma said.

"Where's Uncle Rob now?" I asked.

That's what I called him out loud—even though in my head he was "Soon-to-be Uncle Rob." It's just too long to say, and besides that, he was *almost* related to me. Mom and Dad even called him "Uncle Rob" when they talked about him to Penny and me.

No one answered me. But then Mom said, "So where is Rob?"

"He went to talk to hotel security," Grandma said.

The grown-ups were all standing in a group, talking above our heads.

"I have an idea," Penny whispered to me.

"What?"

"Let's get to a phone and press the Ask Aoife button to find out where Lia is!"

"I don't think that's the kind of thing the

hotel would know," I told her.

"How do you know unless you ask?" Penny said. She did have a point.

Aunt Laura's cell phone buzzed and she answered it quickly. "Hello? Rob?" There was a pause, and then, "Oh, that's great. Thank goodness. We'll see you soon."

When she hung up, she told the rest of us Rob had found Lia, which I'd already figured out just from listening to Aunt Laura's end of the conversation. Lia had gone back up to their hotel room.

Now that everyone was done being worried, there were a bunch of introductions—Rob's relatives who I'd never met. His older brother, Doug, his uncle, who everyone called Chip, even though that didn't sound like a real name, and his dad, another Mr. Perlman. Also his best friend, Noah, was there. There would be more people attending the real wedding. The rehearsal was just for the family—well, family and Noah. Best friends are like family sometimes.

"I wish you could meet the baby!" Grandma said.

"Marco's too young for this kind of trip," Mom explained.

"Nonsense," Grandma said.

"What was that?" Grandpa asked. He wears a hearing aid, but sometimes he turns it off because it whistles a little bit.

"I was just saying it's too bad Marco isn't here!" Grandma practically shouted. It was getting later and later. Aunt Laura picked up her cell phone, then put it down. Picked it up, and put it down.

"Everything is fine," Mom told her. "I'm sure Rob is just talking it out with Lia now."

Finally the ballroom doors opened. Aunt Laura rushed toward Rob and Lia, and the rest of us followed behind her. I'd never met Lia before, but I knew it was her, because she was the only kid with Soon-to-be Uncle Rob.

Rob came over and hugged Mom, Dad, Penny, and me. "Sorry for the delay," he told us. "Lia, come meet your new aunt and uncle and cousins."

This was it—the moment I was finally meeting my soon-to-be cousin.

We stared at each other. Lia had curly hair and a sprinkling of freckles across her nose. Lucky. I've always wanted curly hair and freckles.

I saw Soon-to-be Uncle Rob nudge her. "Hi," she said.

"Hi," Penny and I said back.

Since we were running so late, Aunt Laura and Soon-to-be Uncle Rob decided to cut down a lot of the rehearsing parts of the wedding. They just pointed out where things would go, and showed Penny, Lia, and me where we'd have to stand, then walk, then stand again. Afterwards we'd all go back down the aisle and into another room for snacks and drinks, while the hotel staff cleaned up the ballroom and got it ready for the big party afterward.

"Time for dinner!" Grandma called. We got

back in the elevator and went all the way up, past the twenty-first floor, past a whole bunch of other floors, to the tippy-top of the hotel.

I thought twenty-one floors was high up, but this was practically being in the sky. My ears got clogged and I moved my mouth like a yawn to try and open them.

"Being in a hotel is like being in a city," Penny said as we walked into the restaurant. "Everything you need is all in one place. If we moved here, I don't think we'd ever have to leave."

"Congratulations, Mr. and Mrs. Perlman," the host said. He was wearing the same Hotel Aoife uniform, and I read his name to myself: Jeffrey.

He knew about the wedding. People at this hotel knew *everything*!

"They're not married yet," Lia spoke up.

"We will be tomorrow," Soon-to-be Uncle Rob said.

"Well, come this way," Jeffrey said. He led us through the restaurant, past a smaller version of the fountain downstairs (no fish in this one), past a big, huge salad bar, and past all the other tables, to a small room in the back. There were only two tables in it— one big table set for nine people, and one little table set for three. That was twelve people total, which was exactly how many people were in our party, which meant the room was private, just for us. No other restaurant customers allowed.

I'd never had a private room in a restaurant before, unless you count the party room at Batts Confections. Which I don't, because we've been there so many times, and our store isn't a real restaurant. If you want to eat something that's not candy, like pizza, you have to order it from somewhere else.

Having the room be private wasn't even the best thing. The best thing was that it had windows on three sides, just like the elevator. And instead of looking out at the hotel, it looked out on all of Los Angeles! Since it was getting late, it was dark outside. The city lights were twinkling below.

"As soon as you're seated," Jeffrey said, "I'll take your drink orders."

Penny said, "I claim the seat by the window!" even though every seat was by the window. Anyway there were name tags at each seat, so everyone knew where to sit.

I found mine right at the little table. "I can keep this, right?" I asked, holding up my name tag. I liked the way my name looked spelled out in fancy script.

"Of course," Aunt Laura said.

"Me too?" Penny asked. She can't read too many words yet, since she's just five, but she can read her own name, and she held up her name tag. Aunt Laura nodded, and Penny said, "Goody!"

We all sat down. The little table was for us three kids. Lia was right in the middle of Penny and me. Probably Aunt Laura did that so we could get to know her, but I was feeling a bit shy. It's weird to be shy when you're so excited about something, but sometimes it just happens that way.

But Penny wasn't feeling shy. "We made a song," she said. "As a present for Aunt Laura, and I guess for your dad, too. It goes like this: We're going to be flower girls, flower girls. All three of us will be wearing pearls, wearing pearls." She paused and looked at me. "Sing the next part, Stella."

I looked at Lia. I could tell she didn't like the song. Suddenly it seemed too babyish and not a good present at all. I shook my head.

"We can teach you later, Lia," Penny went on. "You're our first cousin, you know. Our dad is an only child, and Aunt Laura doesn't have any other kids."

"I have lots of cousins," Lia told her. "On my mom's side. So they're not related to you. Do you want to see a picture of my mom?"

"Sure," Penny said.

Lia pulled a photo out of her pocket and handed it over. Penny looked at it, then showed it to me. Lia's mom was pretty. She had the same curly hair as Lia. I didn't see any freckles, but freckles don't always show up in pictures.

I handed the photo back to Lia.

"It's cool that we have our own table," Penny said. "A table just for the flower girls."

"Dad and Laura didn't even ask me if I wanted to be a flower girl," Lia said. "They just told me that's what I'm being."

Hmm, come to think of it, no one asked me either, I thought. One day Mom just said, *Guess what—Aunt Laura's getting married, and you girls get to be the flower girls!*

"I think I should've been given a choice, don't you?" Lia asked.

"I would definitely pick being a flower girl if someone asked me," Penny said. "You get to walk down the aisle just like a bride and wear a pretty dress. My mom says she's never seen such pretty flower-girl dresses before."

"My mom didn't get to see my dress," Lia said. "It's been at my dad's house this whole time, so only he's seen it. Oh, and Laura's seen it." She made a face like she'd tasted something bad.

"Girls," Mom called from the other table, "the waiter will be here soon to take our orders. Did you decide what you want?"

We hadn't even looked yet. But I knew what I wanted. The salad bar. When I said it, that's what Penny said she wanted too. And

I don't think it was just to copy me, because salad bars are so good, of course, she'd want it. Lia wanted it, too. None of the grown-ups did, but grown-ups eat weird things sometimes, like clams and salmon and other fishy things.

After the waiter came and got everyone's orders—all the grown-ups' orders, that is—Grandma walked us to the salad bar.

I'm allergic to lettuce, but not really, I just don't like it. So you'd think I wouldn't like salad bars. But I LOVE them. Because they have way more than just lettuce. They have cheese and tomatoes and carrots and hard-boiled eggs. They have gross things too, like chickpeas and onions and raw broccoli. But you don't have to take anything you don't like. And the stuff you do like, you can take as much as you want.

If I ever own a restaurant, it's definitely

going to have a salad bar.

Penny took avocados, chicken, and red peppers. I piled my plate high with two different kinds of grated cheese—cheddar and mozzarella—and so many cherry tomatoes I didn't even count them. I also got an egg, and plenty of croutons. Lia scooped lettuce onto her plate—yuck, but I didn't tell her that— along with carrots and cucumbers, and some cold pasta.

We brought the salads back to the private room. The grown-ups were being served their appetizers. We finished our salads and went back for seconds—that's another great thing about salad bars—you can always go back for more. Then Penny got tired. While Dad ate, she climbed onto his lap and fell asleep. I wasn't tired at all, just then. Neither was Lia. We're older, so that's why. So then it was just us two at the cousins/flower girls' table.

"Do you think there will be a salad bar at the wedding tomorrow?" I asked.

Lia shook her head. "They're having chicken in a cream sauce tomorrow," she said. "But I'm not having any."

"Are you ordering room service or something?"

Lia shook her head. She looked over at the grown-ups' table, then she lowered her voice. "I'll tell you if you promise not to tell anyone else."

"I promise."

"I'm your cousin, right? Your only cousin, so you have to keep the promise. This will just be our secret, right?"

"I pinky swear," I said.

We hooked pinkies.

"I'm not going at all," she said.

"But—" I started.

"Shh," she warned.

"But why?" I asked in my super softest voice.

"Because I don't want my dad to get married," she said. "Unless he wants to marry my mom again—that'd be okay. But he wants to marry Laura. He says if I give her a chance, I'll love her as much as he does."

"Maybe you will," I said.

Lia shook her head. "No, I won't. You wouldn't want your dad to marry anyone but your mom, would you?"

She was right. I wouldn't.

"Maybe I can't stop him," Lia continued. "But I don't have to watch it if I don't want to," Lia said. "So that's my secret. Now that you know, you can skip it with me."

CHAPTER 4

Thinking About Being Generous

"You look pensive," Dad told me the next morning. "Do you know what that word means?"

I shook my head. Usually I like learning new words. But right then I was busy thinking.

"It means you have a lot on your mind," he said.

Well, that made perfect sense.

"It's because I do," I told him.

"Anything you want to talk about?"

I shrugged my shoulders. I couldn't talk about the thing I wanted to talk about, because I'd pinky-sweared to Lia that I wouldn't.

At dinner last night, while the grown-ups ate dessert and Penny slept on Dad's lap, Lia had told me her secret plan for us to skip the wedding. We would wake up and act normal. We'd get dressed in our flower-girl dresses

just like we were supposed to. We would go down to Ballroom A with our parents. When we got there, we would meet up and sneak off somewhere else, just the two of us. "It won't be either of our hotel rooms," Lia had said. "Because that's the first place they'll look for us, and then they'll just drag us back downstairs and we'll have to go to the stupid wedding anyway."

Lia had also said that she hadn't come up with our exact hiding place yet, but she was going to think about it overnight and let me know when she saw me.

Maybe she'd just been kidding. I really, REALLY hoped so.

But she hadn't sounded like she'd been kidding. She *sounded* like she really, REALLY didn't want her dad to get married again.

"Dad?" I said now.

"Yes, darling?"

"Would you ever marry anyone else?"

"I'm already married to your mother," Dad said.

"I mean if you weren't married to Mom anymore. Like Lia's dad isn't married to her mom anymore."

I hadn't pinky-sweared not to talk about that—and anyway, it wasn't a secret about Lia's parents. Everyone knew it.

"You know, Stel, sometimes people don't get it right the first time around, and it's sad. I'm sure it was very sad for Lia when her parents divorced. But you don't have to worry about Mom and me."

"You got it right the first time?"

"We sure did."

Phew. That was good.

"Dad?" I said again.

"Yes, darling?"

"Do you like Lia?"

"I didn't get to talk to her much," Dad said. "But she seemed sweet, so yes, I like her. Most of all, I liked that the two of you seemed to be getting along so well at dinner last night. It must be nice to finally have a cousin, huh?"

"Yeah," I said. "But maybe I shouldn't spend all my time with her today. I don't want to make Penny feel left out."

"It's nice that you're thinking of your sister," Dad told me. "Penny was fine last night—she got to sit with you and Lia at dinner and I don't think she felt left out. She only came to our table when she was too tired to keep up with the big girls any longer. But she'll have more energy today, and you can spend time with Penny and Lia at the same time."

I couldn't spend time with them both if Lia and I sneaked off and skipped the wedding!

"Your mom and I are so proud of what a generous girl you are," Dad went on.

"Generous?" I asked.

"Yes," he said. "You don't have to spend money to be generous. I mean that you're generous with your heart, which is much more important. Just the idea that you wanted to get something for Aunt Laura was generous, and your concern for Penny is generous. Lia doesn't have a sister, and it was probably sad for her when her parents split up. But she's getting some terrific new family members this weekend. With your generosity of heart, I'm sure she'll think you're the best cousin ever."

Did that mean I was supposed to skip the wedding with her, because that's what Lia wanted?

Dad pulled his cell phone out of his pocket. "I'm just going to call Mrs. Miller to check on her and your brother," he said.

"Stella!" Penny called from the bathroom. "Come quick!"

I raced into the bathroom. Penny was in there with Mom. She had on one of the hotel bathrobes. But it was grown-up sized, not for kids, so the belt part hung down around her knees, and the bottom dragged on the floor.

"I need you to brush your teeth before you put on your dress," Mom told me. "I don't want you to accidentally spit toothpaste on it."

"And there's something I need you to do, too," Penny said. "Look." She pointed to the wall.

"That's the hair dryer," I said. I'd already seen it when Penny and I had first toured the hotel room, and every time I'd used the bathroom since. Unlike other hair dryers, this one was in a plastic case that was attached to the wall.

"Pull it out and turn it on," Penny said.

"Why?"

"Just do it." She glanced over at Mom and then added, "Please."

I reached over and pulled on the handle. It popped out and whoosh, it turned on without my even having to press a button.

"It does that all by itself," Penny said. "Isn't it cool?"

"Uh huh," I said. "How do I turn it off?"

"Just put it back in," she said. "Here, I'll do it for you." She grabbed it from me and pressed it back into the wall case. "I wish we could have one at our house. But we only have a regular hair dryer."

"Girls, come on," Mom said in her impatient voice. "It's teeth-brushing time. We have to get down to the bridal suite to help Aunt Laura get ready in the next twenty minutes."

We'd set our toothbrushes to dry in coffee mugs last night—there were coffee mugs *in the bathroom*!

I took my toothbrush out and squeezed some toothpaste on—the toothpaste we'd brought from home, not the hotel toothpaste, because I was saving it.

"One sec," Penny said, and she opened up the little box with her shower cap in it, and put it on.

"You don't need that," Mom told her.

"Oh yes, I do," she said. "I don't want to get toothpaste in my hair and mess it all up."

When we finished brushing our teeth, it was time to get dressed. I was getting nervous. The closer we got to the wedding, the closer I got to having to decide whether to skip it with Lia. Mom gave me a fresh new pair of tights to wear. I put them on like I was moving in sloooooow motion. Right foot first, super slow.

"Hurry up, Stel," Mom said. "We don't want to keep Aunt Laura waiting on her special day."

I put my left foot into the left foot hole of my tights, just a little bit faster than I did the right foot.

"I think you're going for a world record for the eight-year-old who took the longest time getting ready for her first stint as a flower girl," Dad said.

"And I was fastest," Penny said. She was sitting on the bed, swinging her legs, her tights all pulled up. "Right?"

"Will you be mad if I'm not a flower girl?" I asked.

"Why wouldn't you be a flower girl?" Penny asked.

"Stel," Mom said, "are you scared?"

I nodded, but I didn't say what I was scared of, because then I'd be telling Lia's secret.

"Oh, sweets, you don't have to be scared of being in the wedding," Mom said. "The truth is, everyone in the audience is going to be looking at Aunt Laura, because she's the bride. You and Penny will look beautiful, and I know you'll do a great job, but the bride always gets the most attention."

"Does that make it a little easier, knowing your job isn't quite so big?" Dad asked.

Hmm . . . if my job wasn't so big, maybe it'd be okay to skip it. "A little easier," I said.

"Good," Dad said.

"And Dad and I will be so proud of you for doing something that scared you—because I know that's not an easy thing," Mom added.

I finished putting on my tights. I put on my shiny black shoes. Mom got a little teary and said Penny and I looked beautiful. Dad said Mom also looked beautiful, and he had the three of us stand together so he could take a picture.

Then Mom said it was time to go. "All right, Dave," she said to Dad. "We'll see you later."

Dad wasn't coming to the bridal suite with us because there were no boys allowed—especially not Soon-to-be Uncle Rob. That's because it's bad luck for the groom to see the bride before the wedding.

"See you, Dad," Penny said.

"See you," I echoed.

"But I'll meet up with you before the ceremony," he told me. "And even if the rest of the crowd is looking at Aunt Laura, I'll be looking at you. You and Penny—my girls. So if you start to feel nervous, all you have to do is look over at me."

"Or at me," Mom added.

"Or at Mom," Dad continued. "And know we're right there with you, rooting for you, and proud of you for doing yet another generous thing."

"What's that?" I asked.

"Getting up there and doing something you're scared to do, because you know it means a lot to Aunt Laura."

Uh-oh. How was I going to be able to be generous to Aunt Laura and Lia at the same time?

CHAPTER 5

Something Always Goes Wrong

When we got to the bridal suite, Aunt Laura was already there with her two best friends, Evonne and Nicole, who had arrived that morning, plus Grandma, *plus* a lady doing her hair. She didn't have to go to a salon for her hair—it was right there in the bridal suite!

Aunt Laura's wedding gown was hanging up on the doorframe to the bedroom. It was all puffed out, so it looked like there was already a person inside of it. Except there was no head on top, so it was like a ghost.

"Hello! Hello!" everyone called, beckoning us into the room. There were a lot of hugs. Here's something I learned about weddings: even if people don't know you, they still hug you hello instead of shaking your hand.

On the far side of the room, there was a long table with all sorts of breakfast-y foods, like bagels and croissants and fruit, and those little cereal boxes that are meant for one person, not to share. It was like a breakfast salad bar.

Penny made a run for the cereal boxes, grabbing a mini box of Lucky Charms, and another box of Fruit Loops.

"Easy on the sugar, Pen," Mom said.

"Oh, Elaine, it's a special occasion," Grandma said.

"And be careful of your dresses, girls," Mom added, ignoring Grandma. She said girls, even though it was just one girl— Penny—who even reached for a snack, and I knew better than to spill anyway. "Your one job is to keep those dresses clean."

"I thought our one job is to be flower girls," Penny said.

"Okay, you have two jobs."

"Do you want some cereal too, Stella?" Penny asked. I shook my head. I wasn't hungry. I was nervous.

"Where's Lia?" I asked.

"She's getting ready upstairs," Aunt Laura said. "I hope she comes down soon. I'd like her to be in the 'getting ready' pictures."

That's when Aunt Laura's friend Evonne lifted up her camera and pointed it Aunt Laura's way. Click. "Oh, that was a good one,"

Evonne said. "Doesn't she look beautiful?"

Mom got teary again, and said, "Oh yes, Laura, you're the most beautiful bride ever."

"She doesn't even look like a bride yet because she's not in her dress," Penny pointed out. Aunt Laura was in a robe—a hotel robe just like the one Penny had been wearing, except it actually fit Aunt Laura.

"The wedding gown goes on last," Jennifer said. Jennifer was the lady doing Aunt Laura's hair. Right then she was winding a strand of Aunt Laura's hair around a curling iron. "That way nothing will stain it."

Jennifer put the curling iron down, and then arranged the curls on top of Aunt Laura's head. Her hair looked good and puffy. Wouldn't putting the dress on after make her hair smush back down? It's not like brushing your hair or using a curling iron would do anything to stain a dress. But I didn't say anything. I was still being pensive, about Lia.

She was my new cousin. That meant if I had to choose, I should be generous to her, right?

"Come here, Stel," Aunt Laura said. I stepped toward her. She reached out an arm and squeezed me to her side.

"Stay steady," Jennifer told her.

"Sorry," Aunt Laura said. "It's hard to stay steady when all I want to do is hug one of my two favorite nieces."

"We're your only nieces," I pointed out. "So we're also your least favorites."

"Nope," Aunt Laura said. "You're only my most favorites. Come here too, Pen." She reached out her other arm to pull Penny in. "I'm just so glad you're both here!"

Click, click, click, went Evonne's camera.

She told Mom and Grandma to join us, so they could be in the photos, too. "Say cheese!" Evonne called.

"Cheese!" we all said.

"That was a great one," Evonne said. "You guys look great together. I'll take a bunch at the actual wedding, too."

I clicked my heels together three times and said in my head: *Please let Lia have just been kidding about the wedding skipping stuff.*

"Are you okay, Stel?" Grandma asked.

"Yeah. Why?"

"You're fidgeting so much."

"I was worried you wouldn't be able to come," Aunt Laura said.

"What are you talking about?" Mom asked her.

"Oh, you know, wedding jitters," Aunt Laura said. "I worried something would go wrong—that the baby would get a cold, and you'd have to stay home, or that there'd be a storm and everyone would arrive late."

Here's another thing I learned about weddings: aside from more hugs, there are also more worries.

"Everything's going to be perfect," Nicole said.

"Oh, something will go wrong," Grandma said. "Something always does. But it'll be a little thing, and in the end, it won't matter, because all the people you love most in the world will be here to see you get married."

I knew at that moment I couldn't go through with Lia's plan. I couldn't do that to Aunt Laura. Even if Lia was my new cousin. I'd known Aunt Laura much longer, so that meant that if I had to choose, I had to be generous to her.

At least I was pretty sure that's what it meant.

"Hey, girls, step back and watch this," Jennifer said. We stepped back. She shook a can of hair spray and held up a curly strand of Aunt Laura's hair. Then she aimed the can and sprayed. *Whoosh!* That piece of Aunt Laura's hair turned blue!

I couldn't help but squeal. It was no wonder Jennifer didn't let Aunt Laura put her dress on first!

"You didn't think I'd have plain hair at my own wedding, did you?" Aunt Laura asked.

Actually that's exactly what I'd thought. But I didn't say that out loud. I just shook my head. Now I was speechless!

Penny said, "I didn't know brides were allowed to have colored hair."

"Well, of course, they are," Jennifer said. "I do hair for brides all the time, and they're allowed to do anything with their hair that they want! In fact, blue hair in particular is encouraged. Gets that 'something blue' taken care of."

"Something blue?" Penny asked.

"It's part of a rhyme," Mom explained. "What a bride should wear for luck at her wedding: 'Something old, something new, something borrowed, and something blue.'"

"What are your other things?" I asked.

"For 'something old,' I have the earrings your mom wore to her wedding. They were new back then, but they're old now."

"Thanks a lot," Mom said. Her voice was sarcastic, but she said it with a smile.

Aunt Laura smiled, too. "'Something new' is this dress," she continued. "For 'something borrowed,' there are your mom's earrings again."

"That's double counting!" I said.

"Don't worry," she said. "I'm not aware of any rules against double counting. And now for 'something blue,' there's the hair."

Jennifer lifted a couple more of Aunt Laura's curls and gave a last spray. "What do you think?" Jennifer asked.

"Oh, it's perfect, thank you," Aunt Laura said. "It's even better than I thought it would be."

"Yeah, I love it," I said.

"Me too," Penny piped up.

"I have time to do the girls' hair too, if they want," Jennifer said.

"Really?" I asked.

"Sure thing, as long as your mom says it's okay."

"Please, Mom," Penny said.

"Don't worry, it washes out," Jennifer told her.

"All right," Mom said. Then she added, "But, Jennifer, when it comes to the girls' hair, I think less blue spray is more."

"You got it," Jennifer said. Penny claimed going first, so I watched. I think Mom would've wanted to watch too, just to make sure our hair wasn't made too blue, but she had to go help Aunt Laura put on her dress.

First Jennifer wrapped a towel around Penny's dress so it wouldn't get ruined. Then she unbraided Penny's hair, but kept it divided into three sections. She sprayed blue onto one of the sections, and then she rebraided the braid, so the blue weaved in and out. "I love it!" Penny said.

Then it was my turn. My hair still wasn't long enough for a braid so I was just wearing it down. Jennifer clipped up the sides of my hair. She sprayed the section in the left clip with blue, so I had one blue streak dangling down, next to the rest of my plain brown hair. It looked super cool. Evonne took more pictures.

"Ooh, Stella, Penny! Look at you girls!" Aunt Laura cried, when she and Mom came back out.

"Look at *you*," Evonne said to Aunt Laura. "You look stunning."

Aunt Laura did look stunning. Her dress looked even better on her that it had on the hanger, because Aunt Laura is so much prettier than an invisible ghost.

"I'm going to cry off all my makeup before the ceremony even starts," Aunt Laura's friend Nicole said.

"*Now* you're the most beautiful bride," Penny declared. She ran over to Aunt Laura. *Click*, went Evonne's camera.

"What do you think of our hair?" I asked Mom. The last time Penny had blue hair was when we made a hopscotch court at our friend Maverick's house. But we didn't have paintbrushes, so we used the ends of Penny's braids. When Mom saw, we got punished.

"I think it's perfect for Aunt Laura's wedding," she said.

"I can do yours too," Jennifer offered.

But Mom shook her head. "No, thank you," she said.

We still had a bit of time before going downstairs to the actual wedding, so Aunt Laura showed Penny and me the flowers we'd have. It made me feel like I really was a flower girl. I loved my dress and my hair. I loved being in all the pictures with Aunt Laura. And I loved the flowers, too. There was a big bouquet of roses and lilacs for her, the bride. With Aunt Laura's blue hair, the lilacs seemed to change color, from lavender to sky blue. Penny and I each had a basket of white rose petals. We were going to walk down the aisle ahead of Aunt Laura and throw the rose petals, so the aisle would be all decorated by the time it was her turn.

There was another basket for Lia, too. Aunt Laura dialed Soon-to-be-Uncle Rob and asked for his ETA. She said each letter

separately, like she was spelling it.

"What does E-T-A mean?" I asked Mom.

"Estimated time of arrival," Mom told me. She turned to Aunt Laura as Aunt Laura hung up the phone. "So?"

"Just a few more minutes," Aunt Laura reported.

Penny was swinging her flower petal basket back and forth, back and forth. "Careful, you don't want the petals to fall out," I told her.

"I know," she said, but she stopped swinging it right then, so maybe she didn't really know until I told her. "I claim walking down the aisle first."

"What if the three girls walk down the aisle at the same time?" Grandma said. "That way Aunt Laura is the only one stepping on the petals."

Three girls—that meant Lia, too. She had to have been kidding about skipping the wedding. She just had to.

"Let's practice!" Penny said. The grown-ups watched as we walked down an imaginary aisle. First I was on the left side and she was on the right. Then she was on the right and I was on the left.

"For the real thing, I should be in the middle, between you and Lia, because I'm the youngest," Penny said.

There was a knock on the door. It started to open, and I heard a man's voice—Soon-to-be Uncle Rob's voice—"Everyone decent in there?"

"Don't come in!" we shouted. "It's bad luck!"

Lia walked right in. I saw Soon-to-be Uncle Rob peeking his head in, but then

Penny waved a finger at him. He ducked out and we closed the door.

Lia was all dressed up in the same flower-girl dress as Penny and me. Plus she had a little purple purse with her. There were more hugs, of course. Except Lia didn't hug the people she didn't know. She shook their hands. Maybe she didn't know the wedding rules. But that was okay. Not everyone needs to be huggy.

She hugged Penny and me. "Hey, Cuz," Penny said. "Now we're all twins!"

"Triplets," I corrected.

I wanted to ask Lia if she was kidding about the skipping the wedding thing. But I couldn't ask right in front of everyone else.

Lia pulled on my arm, and whispered into my ear. "I was just thinking, we can't run away yet, because it gives them too much time to find us. So keep acting normal, and when we go downstairs to the ballroom, we'll say we're going to the bathroom together, okay? Then I'll take you to the secret hiding spot I found. It's perfect. No one will ever find us!"

She wasn't kidding. My heart started to beat faster and faster. When should I tell Lia I wasn't going with her, and how should I say it?

"You guys, I'm waiting! Come on!" Penny called. "Okay, I'm going to count to three, and we'll go. We need to practice walking all together. Okay? Okay, Lia?"

"Sure, okay," Lia said.

"One. Two. Three." We each stepped forward, and walked down the pretend aisle, toward where all the grown-ups were standing, smiling at us.

The can of blue hairspray was right on the side table where Jennifer had left it. But I wasn't paying attention to it. I was being pensive again. Maybe when we got downstairs and Lia said she had to go to the bathroom, I'd just say I didn't have to go. I'd stay in the ballroom and be a flower girl, like I was supposed to.

But I knew Lia was going to be mad at me about that.

That's what I was thinking when suddenly I walked straight into the side table—ouch!— and the spray can got knocked off. It rolled onto the floor right in front of us. I fell right over it, and a streak of blue came shooting out.

"Stella!" Mom shouted. But it was too late.

CHAPTER 6

Click

The blue paint had hit Aunt Laura's beautiful white wedding dress. Just below the waist, there was a big dot of blue, with some drips dripping down. It is like the way hot caramel drips down the sides of an ice-cream cone. If caramel came in electric blue, that is.

For a second I couldn't even speak.

"Oh no!" Penny said.

"I'm sorry," I said, finding my voice. "I'm sorry, Aunt Laura. I didn't mean for this to happen."

Jennifer started apologizing, too. "It's my fault. I should've put the cap back on the can. I shouldn't have left it out in the open like that at all."

Evonne put down her camera and ran into the bathroom. I heard the water running, and then she ran back in with a wet towel, and started blotting Aunt Laura's dress. "No, stop," Mom said. "It's not coming out. It's just making the blue part spread out."

"Aunt Laura," I started again.

"I know you didn't mean for this to happen," she said. "It's okay." But I could tell she didn't really think it was, because her voice was hoarse, and her eyes were getting bigger and rounder, like she was going to cry. "Excuse me a sec," she said, and she went into the bathroom. Evonne dropped the towel, and she and Nicole went after her.

That's when *I* started crying. Because I'd never made a grown-up cry before, and Aunt Laura was one of my favorite grown-ups in the whole entire world. "Mom, I'm so sorry," I told her. "I didn't mean for it to happen."

"I knew Uncle Rob shouldn't see the bride before the wedding!" Penny said.

"Mom?" I said.

"It's all right, Stel," she said. "It's just that every bride has a vision for her big day, and this wasn't what Aunt Laura expected."

I'd had a vision for this day, too. And it was nothing like I'd expected either. Not at all.

"Girls, I have an idea," Grandma said. She was talking to Penny, Lia, and me, plus Mom, because to Grandma, Mom is a girl, too. "Elaine, why don't you help Laura out, and I'll take these three downstairs. We can

give everyone up here some space to calm down, and we can check out the ballroom while we're at it. Is that okay with everyone?"

Everyone nodded. At the elevators, Penny told me I could be the one to press the button for the lobby, but I shook my head. "That's okay," I told her. "You can do it." Nothing was going to make me feel better.

We got downstairs, and walked around the fountain, toward the stairs that head toward the ballroom. "Dad!" Penny called out. "Daddy!"

When I looked up, there was Dad rushing toward the concierge desk.

The four of us went right over to him. There was a woman named Julie at the desk. Obviously I knew her name because of her uniform. "What's going on?" Grandma asked.

"There's a problem with the cake," Dad

said. "When the caterers were unpacking it this morning, it had broken, and they're saying there's no way to fix it."

Oh no, that beautiful cake, broken. Could it have happened in the car? Maybe it was my fault too, because I'd bumped into it.

"Uncle Rob strikes again!" Penny said.

"Now, now," Grandma told her. "That's just a silly superstition."

"Is Aunt Laura going to have to have a ruined cake?" A ruined cake, I thought, along with a ruined wedding gown.

"I'm trying to see what the hotel can provide for us," Dad said.

"It's a bit hard to get a wedding cake at the last minute," Julie said.

"You can't know for sure it's just a superstition about Uncle Rob," Penny said. "Because lots of bad things are happening."

But it wasn't because of Uncle Rob. It was because of me.

"Lots of bad things?" Dad asked.

"It's a long story," Grandma told him. "I'm sure Elaine will tell you all about it later. Come on, girls, let's go to the ballroom. Need to stop at the bathroom on the way?"

"Nope," said Penny.

I looked at Lia. "No," she said. I shook my head, too.

The doors to Ballroom A were propped open wide. People were milling around in front, including Grandpa, and Rob's brother, uncle, and dad.

"Is your hearing aid on?" Penny asked Grandpa.

"What?" Grandpa asked, and then he laughed and gave Penny a hug.

The grown-ups were all talking, and, of course, there were more hugs. I glanced around them so I could see into the room—I'd been expecting it to look just as plain and beige as the night before, but it looked completely different! There were rows and rows of chairs. And not the plain chairs, but chairs with pretty flowered cushions on them. Down the middle was a long white satin pathway, leading up to a little platform with tons of purple flowers all around it. The flowers matched the ones in Aunt Laura's bouquet.

Up in the front of the room, a man sat

down at the grand piano, and started playing it. The guests started to take their seats. They didn't know about what had just happened.

"Is the wedding going to be canceled now?" Lia asked.

"Oh no, you don't need to worry about that," Grandma told her.

"What about Aunt Laura?" I asked.

"She'll be here soon," Grandma said. "You don't need to worry either, Stella."

But I was worried, about so many things. What if Aunt Laura's dress looked awful? What if she was mad at me? What if she didn't even want me around?

"I have to go to the bathroom," Lia said.

"I thought you didn't have to go," Grandma said.

"That was then. But I have to go now— and I can't hold it."

"All right, let's go," Grandma said. "We'll make it quick."

"No, you don't have to," Lia said. "You have lots of people to talk to. Stella can come with me. Right, Stella?"

She was looking at me. And I was looking at her.

And right then, I decided.

"Yeah," I said. "I can go with Lia."

"Me too!" said Penny.

I saw Lia's eyes flash. But there wasn't anything I could do. If I told Penny she wasn't allowed to come, Grandma would want to know why.

I think Lia knew it too, because she didn't say anything. Grandma said we could go to the bathroom all together. I followed Lia down the hall, and Penny followed me. We rounded the corner and went into the

bathroom. Penny headed into the first stall. I
started to walk into the stall next to hers, but
Lia held my arm. She waited until we heard
Penny lock her stall door, and then she pulled

me back out into the hall and started to run.

"Come on!" she said.

I hesitated for a second. "But Penny," I said.

"Come *on,*" Lia said.

"Okay," I said. Back out into the hall we went. Lia was running, and I was running after her, and behind me there was a voice calling, "Stella! Stella, wait!"

Oh no! It was Penny!

I had to slow down and let her catch up. "I thought you were waiting for me in the bathroom," she said.

"I know a better one," Lia said. "An even fancier one. Come on!" We followed her into a stairwell, and down a flight of stairs. At the bottom, Lia pushed open the stairwell door. We were in a hallway that didn't even look like we were still in the same hotel.

"Here it is," Lia said. She pulled open a plain white door, and ushered us inside. The door shut behind us.

Click.

CHAPTER 7

Something Blue

It was dark for a second, but then Lia flicked a light switch, and the room got bright.

"Room" was the wrong word for where we were. It was more like a closet. Not the kind you keep coats in, but the kind with a bunch of shelves, and all sorts of supplies. On one side, there were buckets and mops and cleaning things, as well as cans with weird labels, like "pellets" and "bloodworms."

Bloodworms?! EWWWWW!

"I don't like this place," Penny said, her voice shaky. She couldn't even read well enough to see the word "Bloodworms." If she did, she'd like it even less. "This isn't fancy. This isn't even a bathroom. I need to get out of here."

That's how I felt, too.

Penny turned around to reach for the door. "Hold up," Lia told her. "I'll let you in on a secret. This is our hideout. Our *secret* hideout."

"What is this place really?" I asked.

"It's where they keep the food and supplies for the fish," Lia said.

"We should find a different secret hideout," Penny said. "One that smells better than this one. But we can't do it right now, because right now it's time to go back and be in the wedding."

"That's just it," Lia said. "If we stay in here, in our secret hideout, we don't have to be in the wedding."

"But I want to be in the wedding!" Penny said. "I'm in my special dress, and I have my special flowers—well, Grandma is holding them for me, but they're mine." Penny looked at me. "She has yours, too. Remember we get to sprinkle the petals down the aisle before Aunt Laura walks down?"

"Yeah, I remember," I said.

"And we promised!"

"I didn't promise anything," Lia said. "Stella, did you?"

"Not exactly," I said.

"Yes, you did," Penny said stubbornly. "Because you never told Aunt Laura or Mom that you wouldn't. We've been practicing all morning, and you never told them you were going to run away. That's almost exactly the same thing as breaking a promise. And it's not nice to break a promise, Stella—especially when the person is getting married on that same day."

Penny spoke the last sentence in a voice like I was the younger sister, and she was the older one, trying to teach me the right thing to do.

But I wasn't sure about the right thing. If I kept doing things to ruin the wedding, maybe I shouldn't be in it. Maybe that was the best present to get for Aunt Laura.

Still, Penny should be allowed. She didn't ruin anything, and it's what she wanted to do.

Lia had moved to stand between Penny and the door, so Penny couldn't get out. Penny looked like she was about to cry. I felt bad for her. Even though she's always copying me and it makes me annoyed, I felt bad that she copied me this time and now she was missing out on something she wanted to do.

"She wants to go," I said. "Let her go."

"Okay, fine," Lia said, stepping aside. "But if you leave, you have to promise not to tell anyone where Stella and I are, okay?"

Penny shook her head. I thought she was saying, no, she couldn't make that promise. I wasn't that surprised. Little sisters can be big tattletales sometimes.

But that wasn't it. "I can't find my way back to the ballroom by myself," Penny said. "We took too many turns, and went down stairs, and then there were more turns. You didn't tell me I had to pay close attention and now I don't remember how to go. You have to take me!"

"Okay, I will," I said.

"But—" started Lia.

"I have to," I said. "She's only five years old."

Penny reached forward, twisted the doorknob and tried to push the door open, but she couldn't do it. I put my hand on the doorknob to turn it. But it didn't turn at all. Then I pushed my shoulder against the door, and it still didn't move at all.

"Lia," I said, my heart starting to beat

fast in my chest again, "I think the door is locked."

Lia tried the doorknob, but it stayed frozen in place. She leaned against the door, trying to push it open. "Help me," she said, so Penny and I leaned, too. But it didn't budge. Not even the eensy weensiest bit.

I banged on the door, and Penny banged on the door. "People don't come down this hall," Lia told us. "They just come here when it's time to feed the fish. That's why it's a good secret hideout."

"So we're locked in and no one will hear us? We're going to miss the whole wedding!" Penny said. I put my arm around her. "What if we never get out? Then we'll miss even more! We'll miss the party, and we'll miss going home. We'll miss Mom and Dad and Marco. We'll miss everything!"

I felt the hot feeling that comes behind my eyes right before I start to cry. It's like when you're sucking on a really spicy mint, or accidentally eat a red-hot jelly bean, thinking it's a cherry one. Then the backs of your eyeballs start to get really hot, and the fronts of your eyeballs start to water.

I blinked my eyes quickly and swallowed hard and made myself not cry. I was the big sister—so I had to act brave, even if I wasn't actually feeling brave right then. It was my fault Penny was there. I should've known she'd try to copy me, and go wherever I was going.

"We'll get out," I told Penny. "I promise— and like you said, you're not allowed to break a promise, so I won't break this promise to you. The fish are going to need to eat again, and someone will be sent to get them food. When they do, they'll open this door, and we'll get out. Right, Lia?"

"Right," she said. "Except."

"Except what?" Penny and I asked at the same time. You could tell it was a serious situation, because neither of us said "jinx."

"Except when I called Ask Aoife to ask about when the fish were fed, the woman said it was once a day, first thing in the morning. So it's possible we won't get out until tomorrow."

"Tomorrow?" Penny cried. "That's a whole day away. You mean we have to sleep here? I've never slept without Belinda, my favorite stuffed platypus. And what about food? All there is in here is food for the fish."

I shuddered just thinking about the bloodworms.

"We can't eat fish food!" Penny went on. "We're not Fudge or Penny Jr.! We're people, and we're going to starve!"

There were other things I was scared of, too, like what if we had to go to the bathroom? We didn't have a toilet in here. Just thinking about it made me have to go.

We slid onto the floor.

"I should've checked the door," Lia said. "I just thought if it opened from the outside, it would have to open from the inside, too."

"Poor Aunt Laura," Penny cried. "She really wanted us in the wedding."

"She wanted *you* in the wedding," I said. "But I don't think she wanted me—not anymore, at least."

"I don't think she really wanted me in the wedding either," said Lia.

"Why?" I asked. "She still likes you."

"She only likes me because she likes my dad. But she didn't pick me to be in her family."

"She didn't pick Penny and me either," I said.

"It's different, because you're related," Lia said.

"When they have the wedding, you'll be related too."

"Yeah, I guess," she said. "It's still not quite the same."

Then we were all quiet for a little while.

I wondered what they were doing at the wedding right then. I'm sure Mom and Dad were really worried about us. I hoped they weren't mad at Grandma, since she was in charge of watching us. It wasn't her fault we ran away.

I wished there were a clock in the room, or I wished I were wearing a watch. What time was it? How much time had passed? Was Aunt Laura walking down the aisle right then, or was the wedding already over?

"Aunt Laura doesn't care about things like that," Penny said suddenly.

"Like what?" I asked.

"Like if you're related. She just likes everyone. I bet she likes you, Lia, even if she wasn't marrying your dad."

"You're right," I said. "That's the thing about Aunt Laura. She finds something to like about everyone. There was this one time we were in a store, and the lady on line in front of us was acting super mean, just because the line was taking a long time. It wasn't anyone's fault, but this lady was complaining so loud and making everyone feel bad. Then Aunt Laura told her, 'I love your shoes.' And the lady stopped complaining, just like that."

"Remember that other time when she came to visit? Mom and Dad said they'd made a plan to go to dinner, just grown-ups, and we had to stay home with Mrs. Miller, even though she's old and no fun and smells like cough drops. Aunt Laura told Mom she and Dad should have a date night, and then we got to have a girls' night. You wrote that play, and we acted it out."

"She acted it out, too," I remembered. "Most grown-ups would just want to be in the audience and watch."

"It's kind of like she's not a real grown-up," Lia said. "I mean, my mom would never have blue hair."

"Neither would my mom," I said. "But Aunt Laura's still a grown-up. She's just a different kind of grown-up."

"A really good kind," Penny said.

"She's so different than my mom," Lia said.

"She's different than my mom, too," I said. "They're sisters, and they're still so different."

"But at least your mom gets to be here today," Lia said. "My dad said I couldn't invite my mom to see me in the wedding, because Laura might feel weird about that."

"Did you ask Aunt Laura?" I asked.

Lia shook her head.

"I think you should ask Aunt Laura if it

would be okay," I told her.

"Would you start liking her if she said yes?" Penny asked.

"I guess I would," Lia said. "I sort of like her already—because of the things you said."

"Hooray!"

"Not hooray," Lia said. Her eyes drifted to the closet door, shut and locked. I shifted positions—oops, now I had to go to the bathroom even more.

"Do you think this is all because Uncle Rob saw Aunt Laura before the wedding?" Penny asked.

"If it is, then nothing that happened was my fault after all."

"It wasn't your fault," Lia said. "It was my fault—Laura wanted me to go with her to get ready in the bridal suite, and I said no. But if I'd gone with her like she asked, my dad wouldn't have had to drop me off, and if he hadn't dropped me off, maybe all this bad luck stuff wouldn't have happened, and we wouldn't be locked in here."

" 'Something old, something new, something borrowed, and something blue,' " Penny said.

"I think Aunt Laura shouldn't have doubled up," I said. "Then when Uncle Rob saw her, she didn't have enough luck to save the day."

"But what if we can find that in here?" Penny asked. "Maybe if we gather up our luck all together, the door will unlock."

"It doesn't work that way," I told her.

"How do you know?" Penny asked.

I shrugged my shoulders. It was the kind of thing I just knew—like knowing people can't grow wings and fly, and fish pellets won't turn into candy.

"I'll help you, Penny," Lia offered. "It's not like there's anything else to do."

"Thanks," Penny said. She'd stood up, and now she was running her hands along the shelves. "This looks old," she said, pulling at an old rag that was a little bit ripped and had a lot of stains. Penny held it by the edges—that's how dirty it was. "Now I need something new."

"Our dresses are all new," Lia offered.

"I think we need to find something new that's just from this room," Penny said.

That was just a made-up rule, but I didn't say anything. What if she was right? I didn't want to ruin anything else.

Lia found paper towels that looked brand new—they were still wrapped up in plastic. "And everything is borrowed, so that's all taken care of," she said.

"No, don't double up," I told her. I didn't really believe it, but just in case. That hadn't worked when Aunt Laura had doubled up on something borrowed and something old. "Let's find something to officially borrow, and we'll give it back when we get out of here," I said.

"Ooh, I know," Penny said. "We'll borrow the end of this shelf to put all the stuff we find."

"Great," said Lia.

Now we just needed something blue. Not our hair—because that blue spray was already bad luck. Penny found some cleaning stuff that was a greenish color. "Can we use this?" she asked.

I shook my head.

"It's not really blue."

"I know," said Lia. "How about us?"

"Us?"

"Because we're blue," she said. "Not blue the color—blue the feeling. We're sad. That counts, right?"

"Um," I said. "But doesn't that not count as something we found in this room?"

"It does too count," Penny said. "Because we weren't blue until we got locked in here!"

And right at that same exact moment—I swear this really happened—right then, we heard a click in the lock, and the door swung open.

And guess who was on the other side!

If you're reading this, I'm not really going to make you guess. I'm going to tell you: it was my dad.

CHAPTER 8

Your Presence is Your Present

Dad wasn't alone. Standing next to him, there was a lady in a business suit, and on the other side, a POLICE OFFICER.

"Oh, thank goodness, you're all safe and sound," Dad said. He opened up his arms and we were all crowding into them—even Lia. But then he let go, and held the three of us out at arm's length. "What were you thinking, running off like that? What were you THINKING?!"

Penny started sniffling. "Please don't make me go to jail, Daddy. I'm sorry. I'm really sorry. It wasn't my idea."

Uh-oh, there went my little sister tattle-telling again.

I glanced over at the police officer. He had a walkie-talkie raised up to his mouth, and he said, "They've been found."

I turned back to Dad. "I'm sorry, too," I told him.

"I'm sure you are," he said. "But we're still going to have a family talking-to, just so you know."

That's when I remembered that I really, REALLY had to go the bathroom. I twisted my legs, one around the other. Dad's cell phone rang right then. It was Mom, making sure we'd really and truly been found. Penny grabbed the phone. "Mommy!" she cried.

The lady who'd opened the door said she'd take me to the bathroom. I followed her, even though she was a stranger, and we're not supposed to go anywhere with strangers. She had helped find us—and Dad seemed to trust her. Besides, the police officer was there, and he seemed to think it was okay, too.

She waited right outside the door for me. When I finished, I washed my hands, and she handed me a paper towel. "You kids gave us quite a scare," she said.

"I'm sorry," I said again. "How did you know how to find us?"

"I got a call from a young girl just this morning. She was very curious about the feeding schedule for the koi fish—where the food was kept, what the hours were for my staff going into the storage room to get the food, whether the cleaning crew ever went into that room to clean things up, and how often that happened. When your father called to say the three of you were missing, we notified hotel security. We had everyone looking out for you."

"Even the police," I said.

"Your mom called them," she explained. "They arrived in the ballroom right about the time I did. They were gathering information about you girls, asking for room numbers. Lia's dad, Rob, gave his room number—1104— and that's when I remembered the call. It had come in from that very same room. Since Rob himself doesn't have the voice of a young child, I figured it had to be Lia calling, and I figured maybe the reason why she was asking all those questions about the supply closet was because she was planning to run away to it. As soon as I put two and two together, your dad and I raced over—along with Officer Robbins. We opened the door, and you know the rest."

"Thanks for finding us," I told her.

"My dear, it's my job," she said.

"Your job is finding people?" I asked.

"My job is to help people with whatever question or problem they have when they're guests at this hotel."

"Oh, I get it," I said. "You answer the phone for the Ask Aoife hotline—and that's the number that Lia called."

"My dear," the lady said, taking my hand and leading me out the bathroom door, "I *am* Aoife!"

Aoife and I walked back to Ballroom A. My whole entire family was standing together, crowded around Lia and Penny. A bunch of the regular guests were there, too. Penny spotted us first. "Hi, Stella!" she said. "They're not mad anymore—well, only a little bit mad."

She didn't even finish her sentence before Mom, Aunt Laura, Grandma, and Grandpa all rushed toward me and took turns hugging me. "I'm sorry," I told them all—it was the third time I'd apologized since we got out of the closet. But I didn't know what else to say.

"I know you are, honey," Mom said. "Penny and Lia explained everything."

"How could you ever have thought I didn't want you to be in my wedding?" Aunt Laura asked.

"Well," I started, "because you wanted your wedding to be perfect, and I wanted you to have a perfect wedding, but I messed so many things up, and . . ." My voice trailed off, because looking at her dress right then, I didn't see any kind of blue paint on it. "Your dress—it's washed off."

"Not exactly," Aunt Laura said. She lifted up a layer, and revealed a flash of blue paint underneath. "Evonne remembered she'd brought a white shawl along, and she ran up to her room to get it. I put it on and knotted it in the back." She dropped the shawl back down. "Looks good, doesn't it?"

I nodded.

"I think so, too," Aunt Laura said. "When I looked in the mirror, it looked like I'd planned to wear the dress like this all along, so Evonne said she'd loan it to me for the day."

Another something borrowed! That meant nothing was doubled up, after all!

"So now will you be in my wedding?"

"But I thought the wedding already happened," I said.

"Yeah," Lia said. "It was starting right

when we left."

"You think I'd get married without my one and only daughter right there by my side?" Rob asked her.

"Or that I'd get married without her—or without my two favorite nieces?" Aunt Laura added.

"Goody!" Penny cried.

"But I wanted to get you something special that you'd remember the day by, and instead it got all messed up."

"I don't need any present from you," Aunt Laura said. "Your presence is your present. So are we ready to get started?"

"Yes!" said Penny.

I shook my head. "Lia has something to ask you first."

"Lia," Aunt Laura said. "What's your question?"

"Ask her," I prompted.

"Would it be all right if my mom came and got to see me be in this wedding?" Lia asked. "I really want her to see me in my dress and walk down the aisle."

"Oh, Lia," Aunt Laura said. "Of course, that'd be all right."

Lia called her mom, who said she'd be there in an hour. Aoife stepped up to the front of the room. She put her fingers in her mouth and gave the super loudest whistle I've ever heard in my whole entire life. Everyone quieted down right away. She made an announcement that the ceremony was being delayed a little bit, but there'd be champagne for all the grown-ups, and orange juice for the kids in the meantime.

But then Rabbi Wasserman came to talk to Aunt Laura and Soon-to-be Uncle Rob, and

said he couldn't wait for another hour. He had another function to attend. "We've already delayed a while," he explained.

"Not that long," Mom said. "We're only—" she paused to look at her watch—"thirty-five minutes behind schedule."

"Are you sure?" I asked. "It felt like we were gone for way longer than that."

"I'm sure," Mom said. "But believe me, they were the longest thirty-five minutes of my life."

"Mine too," Dad echoed.

"Mine too," Aunt Laura and Uncle Rob said at the same time.

"Jinx," Penny yelled. But then she added, "Briggs Laura" and "Perlman Rob," so the two of them could keep talking.

"Add another hour," said Rabbi Wasserman, "and I just can't do it."

"I guess we can't wait for Mom," said Lia.

"Oh no," Aunt Laura told her. "We're waiting. She should've been on the guest list all along. Right, Rob?"

"Right," he said. "I'm sorry, sweetheart. You were right."

Penny shook her head. "Uncle Rob strikes again!"

"What?" asked Rob. "What'd I do?"

"You keep seeing Aunt Laura before the wedding," Penny told him. "You're standing next to her RIGHT NOW. That's bad luck, you know."

"Bad luck, schmad luck," said Uncle Rob. "You girls are our good-luck charms—I think we'll be all right."

"I don't know how lucky we really are," Lia said, her voice just an eensy bit shaky. "After all, the rabbi is leaving."

"But you'll stick around for the wedding now, whenever it is?" Aunt Laura asked her.

"Yeah," said Lia. "I will. I promise."

Aunt Laura put her arm around Lia's shoulder. "That's all I need to know," she said. "We can have the party now—everyone's here, and ready to celebrate. There's no rule that you can't have the party first, and then get married. If Rabbi Wasserman can't do it today, we'll do it tomorrow. We may not have all our guests still here, but we'll get married. The important thing is the family is still intact."

"A reverse wedding," Mom said. "It's not the traditional route—but then again, my kid sister has never been the most traditional girl."

"This is the one day I actually wanted to be," Aunt Laura said. "I wanted things to be in the right order, and I wanted the kids to walk down the aisle and throw petals, and I wanted Mom and Dad to give me away, in front of all of my friends. But it's okay, you know, as long as the girls are safe and sound. It doesn't really matter how this wedding happens, just as long as it does eventually."

"I guess I should let the guests know," Rob said.

"Know what?" Aoife asked, walking back over to us.

"The rabbi apparently has another function to attend. So we'll have the party now. Whenever he can come back, we'll have him marry us."

"Does it have to be this rabbi who marries you?" Aoife asked.

"I suppose not," Rob said. "It could be a priest, or a justice of the peace."

"Or a hotel proprietor?" asked Aoife.

"Are you trying to tell us that YOU can perform this wedding ceremony?" Mom asked.

"I'm licensed in the state of California," she said.

"Oh, Aoife, thank you," Aunt Laura said. "Thank you so much."

"Wait a second," said Penny. "Your name is Aoife?" I forgot they hadn't been introduced.

"It is," she said.

"You have the same name as the hotel!" Penny told her.

"I know. It's my hotel."

"The whole hotel is yours?" Penny asked, nearly breathless.

"Yup."

"Wow, I didn't know you could have your own hotel. When I grow up, that's what I'm going to do. I'm going to have my own hotel, and also my own candy store, and be a princess, and be a writer."

That was a really long list of things to be, but I didn't say anything, because right then everything seemed possible.

CHAPTER 9

Perfection

An hour later, Lia's mother had arrived, and she was seated along with all the other wedding guests. Someone else from the hotel—a man with the name Peter sewn into his uniform— stood out in the hall with us. From inside Ballroom A, I could hear the organ music playing. Mom told me it was called Pachelbel's *Canon.* (How can grown-ups recognize songs that don't have any words?)

Peter told each of us when to walk down

the aisle. First went Rob and his dad. Penny, Lia, and I peeked through the window on the ballroom door, so we could see Rob get to the front and stand in front of Aoife. His dad sat down in the first row. Then it was time for Mom and Rob's brother, Doug, to walk down—Mom was the matron of honor, and Doug was the best man. Mom gave Penny, Lia, and me each a little kiss, and then Peter opened the door. Everyone was walking SUPER slowly. That's a wedding rule.

My heart was thump thump thumping all over again. Even though Mom and Doug were walking, it was going to be our turn soon enough. In fact we were next! Aunt Laura and Grandma and Grandpa would be the last ones.

"Okay," Peter said. "Get ready, girls."

"Ready!" Penny said.

"I'm ready too," Lia told him.

"Stella?" Peter said. "All set?"

I looked down at my shoes, I smoothed down my dress, I gripped my basket, and I took a deep breath. "Yeah," I said. "I am."

He opened the door.

Everyone in the ballroom turned to look at us, and made the "Awwww" sound.

Lia moved in between Penny and me. She hooked her right arm through Penny's left arm, and her left arm through my right arm. We still had our hands free to hold our flowers and throw the petals. "Let's step forward on our right feet first," she said. "On the count of three."

One, two, three: step!

Right, then pause, left, then pause, then right again. Slowly we made our way down the aisle, sprinkling flower petals as we went.

"Aren't they darling?" I heard someone say, but I didn't look up to see who. I just concentrated on walking. Step and throw petals, step with the other foot and throw petals. We finally got to the end, and the music changed to another song without words. But this one I recognized anyway. It was "Here Comes the Bride."

Aunt Laura walked down the aisle in between Grandma and Grandpa, walking slower than I've ever seen anyone walk in my whole entire life. Aunt Laura looked so pretty. I felt tears pricking behind my eyes. When they got to the end, Aoife said, "Who gives this woman to be married?"

"I do," Grandma said. She nudged Grandpa.

"Oh, sorry," he said. "I do, too."

Aunt Laura handed Lia her wedding

bouquet to hold. "Ladies and gentlemen," Aoife said, "we are gathered here today . . ."

And then the wedding went on, just like a wedding in a movie. To be honest, it got a little bit boring, and my feet started to hurt from standing so long. But then Aoife got to the good part, and it wasn't boring anymore: "Do you, Robert, take Laura to be your lawfully wedded wife, in good times and bad, in sickness and in health, for richer or poorer, until death do you part?"

"I most certainly do," said Rob.

In the front row, I could hear Grandma and Mom sniffling.

"Do you, Laura, take Robert to be your lawfully wedded husband, in good times and bad, in sickness and in health, for richer or poorer, until death do you part?"

"Yes, I do," Laura said.

Everyone started to clap right then, and Aoife had to say, "Hold on, folks, we're not done yet. We need the rings. Best man, can you hand me the rings?"

Doug took the two rings from his jacket pocket. Laura slipped a gold ring around Rob's finger. Rob slipped a smaller, fancier ring around Laura's finger. It had stones of all different colors, so it would match her hair, no matter what color she dyed it.

Doug reached into his pocket and pulled out *another* ring, and handed it to Aunt Laura. She reached out an arm, and pulled Lia toward her. "Lia, do you take me to be your stepmother?" Laura said. "In good times and bad, even though we might not always see eye-to-eye, and sometimes you might find me downright annoying? Even though you already have such a good mom, and I'm

not trying to take her place? But I do hope
you know that I'm going to be the very best
stepmom that I can possibly be."

Lia looked to the audience. I knew she
was looking at her mom. I saw her smile and

give a tiny wave, and then she turned back to Aunt Laura. "I know," she said. "I take you."

"Good," Aunt Laura said, wiping away tears. "I take you, too."

Aunt Laura slipped the ring onto Lia's finger. Then Doug put something in a napkin right behind Rob's foot, and Rob lifted his foot and stomped down right on top of it. There was a smashing sound.

"What is that?" Penny whispered. But all I knew was that it was something breakable, and I shrugged my shoulders.

"It's the glass," Lia explained. "It's a tradition in a Jewish wedding. Now it's broken into lots of teensy tiny pieces, and the myth goes this marriage will last until all the pieces get put back together again."

"They won't, though, right?" Penny asked.

"Nope, they won't," Lia assured her.

"I now pronounce you husband and wife—and stepmother and stepdaughter," Aoife said. "Okay, everyone, now you can clap!" The room erupted in applause.

"Hooray, we're cousins!" Penny cried.

The music started up again. This time Aunt Laura and Uncle Rob (he wasn't Soon-to-be Uncle Rob anymore! Not even in my head!) were the first people to walk down the aisle. The rest of us followed behind them.

"It's party time," Dad said.

Suddenly I knew my question. I turned to look behind me. "Hey, Aoife, can I ask you something?"

"Of course."

"Is there any way you can fix the cake?"

She grinned. "Already done, my dear," she said. "I had one of my chefs turn your one broken cake into five perfect ones."

I skipped to catch up with Aunt Laura. "This was the best wedding ever," I told her. "But I'm still so sorry about your dress."

"I don't care about my dress," she said. "Come with me. You too, Penny, Lia, come along. Rob, you can come too. Everyone, come along!"

Soon we were running through the halls of the hotel, up a stairwell, and out onto the second floor, the floor that smelled like pool. Aunt Laura pressed the double doors at the end of the corridor, and there it was, the indoor swimming pool. It was the biggest pool I'd ever seen, and the water was bright blue. I wished I had my bathing suit right then.

"All right, wedding party, everyone in!" Aunt Laura cried, and she jumped.

She jumped INTO THE POOL! With her WEDDING GOWN ON!

Then Rob jumped in after her. "I can't believe them!" Lia said, but then she jumped, too.

"Wait!" I cried. "What about our clothes?"

"What about them?" Laura called. "We're in a hotel—you have things to change into for later, and do you really think these dresses matter more than this memory? Come in!"

And so we all did. I jumped in. Penny jumped holding Dad's hand. Mom was there, and Rob's brother, Doug, and even Grandma. Grandpa took just enough time to take out his hearing aid, and then he jumped, too.

It was our family jumping into the pool with our clothes on. Well, except for Marco and Fudge and Penny Jr. But I'd tell them all about it. I don't think anyone ever imagined this was what the wedding would be like. But you know what? It was still perfect. My flower-girl dress billowed around me. The purple looked even prettier in the water. "Three flower girls in a pool," Lia sang to the tune of Penny's song. "Isn't that so cool?"

Penny splashed me and I turned toward her. "Knock, knock," she said.

"Who's there?"

"Will you remember this in a second?" she asked.

She was getting Talisa's joke a little bit

wrong, but that was okay. She was only five. And I knew the answer anyway. Aunt Laura was right. My dress didn't matter, but the memory did.

"I'll remember this for my whole entire life," I told her. "Hey, Aunt Laura?"

"Yes, Stel?"

"You know how you said I didn't need to get you a present?"

"Yup—you don't."

"Well, you're getting one anyway. This wedding was so great I'm going to write all about it in a book—my sixth book, and then I'm going to give it to you."

"I can't think of anything I'd ever want more," Aunt Laura said.

So that's what I did.

THE END

P.S. You just finished reading it.

Sneak preview of

Stella Batts

None of Your Beeswax

Book

"I think it's time to feed the fish," I told my friend Lucy.

Penny and I each have a pet goldfish. Mine is named Fudge, and Penny's is named Penny Jr. They both live in little glass bowls on a shelf in the kitchen.

"Can I feed one of them?" Lucy asked.

"Sure," I told her. "You can feed Penny Jr. She's the one in the bowl on the left." Penny and I usually each feed our own fish, but since she wasn't home, I figured Lucy could feed Penny Jr. this time.

"Cool, it'll be my fish for the day!" Lucy said.

Penny Jr. is pure gold—actually orange, like the orange part of a candy corn. My fish, Fudge, has a little fleck of black on his tail. The other way you can tell them apart is that Fudge is a much faster swimmer. Like right then, he was darting all around his bowl, but Penny Jr. was just floating in place.

I got the box of fish food from the pantry, and I showed Lucy how you take just a pinch of the colored flakes between your fingers, and then you sprinkle it gently on top of the water.

Fudge must have felt the water ripple, or smelled the food, or something, because he swam up to the food right away. I like to watch his mouth open up as he sucks in his flakes, like they're the yummiest things in the whole entire world, even though they kind of make your fingers smell bad when you touch them.

"Now your turn," I told Lucy.

Lucy took a pinch of flakes just like I'd showed her. She dropped them right onto the top of the water in Penny Jr.'s bowl.

"Watch her little mouth open up to grab them," I said. We were both standing on the bench by the table, peering over at the bowl. But Penny Jr. didn't do anything besides just keep floating beside them.

"Hmmm," I said. "Maybe you didn't give her enough."

"I did it just like you showed me," Lucy said.

I took another little pinch between my own fingers and dropped it in.

"Hey, that's my fish!" Lucy said. She took another pinch—this one wasn't so little—and dropped a third bit of flakes into the bowl. "Oh, Penny Jr., wake up and smell the fish flakes!"

But nothing happened except that now the top of Penny Jr.'s bowl was full of floating colored flakes, AND a floating Penny Jr.

Come to think of it, fish aren't supposed to float, are they? They're supposed to swim.

Lucy and I realized something about Penny Jr. at the exact same time, and we looked at each other, our eyes as big and round as gumballs.

"Poke it," I told her.

"No, you poke it. It's your fish."

"It's *your* fish," I reminded her.

"Just for the day," she said. "It's your sister's fish really, and that's closer to being your fish than my fish. It's not even in my family. Besides, I don't even want it anymore."

I was afraid to poke Penny Jr. with my finger. There was a pencil on the shelf and I picked it up and tapped it into the water, poking Penny Jr. Just a little poke. Nothing happened, except the water rippled a little bit.

"You can't wake her if you poke too gently," Lucy said.

"You think she's just sleeping?"

"Maybe," she said. "Do fish sleep upside down?"

I didn't think so, but I poked harder this time. Hard enough that Penny Jr. would definitely wake up if she was alive. She was still floating on her back, only now she was bouncing up and down in the ripples, because I'd swished the water with the pencil.

EWWWWWWWWW! I touched a dead fish! With a pencil, but still. I touched a dead fish! I touched a dead fish!

"Dad!" I cried out, so loud I heard Marco wake up and start to cry too.

"Dad!"

"What?" Dad called back.

"Come quick!" I screamed. "Something awful has happened to Penny!"

Courtney Sheinmel

Courtney Sheinmel is the author of several books for middle-grade readers, including *Sincerely* and *All the Things You Are*. Like Stella Batts, she was born in California and has a younger sister. However, her parents never owned a candy store. Now Courtney lives in New York City, where she has tasted all the cupcakes in her neighborhood. She also makes a delicious cookie brownie graham-cracker pie. Visit her at www.courtneysheinmel. com, where you can find the recipe along with information about all the Stella Batts books.

Jennifer A. Bell

Jennifer A. Bell is an illustrator whose work can be found on greeting cards, magazines, and almost a dozen children's books. She lives in Minneapolis, Minnesota, with her husband and son. Visit her online at www. JenniferABell.com.

Praise for Stella Batts:

"Sheinmel has a great ear for the dialogue and concerns of eight-year-old girls. Bell's artwork is breezy and light, reflecting the overall tone of the book. This would be a good choice for fans of Barbara Park's 'Junie B. Jones' books."
— *School Library Journal*

"First in a series featuring eight-year-old Stella, Sheinmel's unassuming story, cheerily illustrated by Bell, is a reliable read for those first encountering chapter books. With a light touch, Sheinmel persuasively conveys elementary school dynamics; readers may recognize some of their own inflated reactions to small mortifications in likeable Stella, while descriptions of unique candy confections are mouth-watering."
— *Publishers Weekly*

Other books in this series:

Meet Stella and friends online at www.stellabatts.com